BEST
WORD BOOK
EVER

THE ALPHABET

The alligator is eating an apple.
The goose is wearing gloves.
What is the xiphias doing?

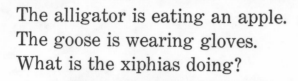

A alligator

B bear

C cat

D dog

E egg

F fish

G goose

H heart

I ice cream cone

J jack-o'-lantern

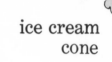

K kangaroo

L letter carrier

M mailbag

N nut

O owl

P present

Q queen

R rug

S spider

T turtle

U umbrella

V vase

W walrus

X xiphias

xylophone

Y yarn

Z zipper

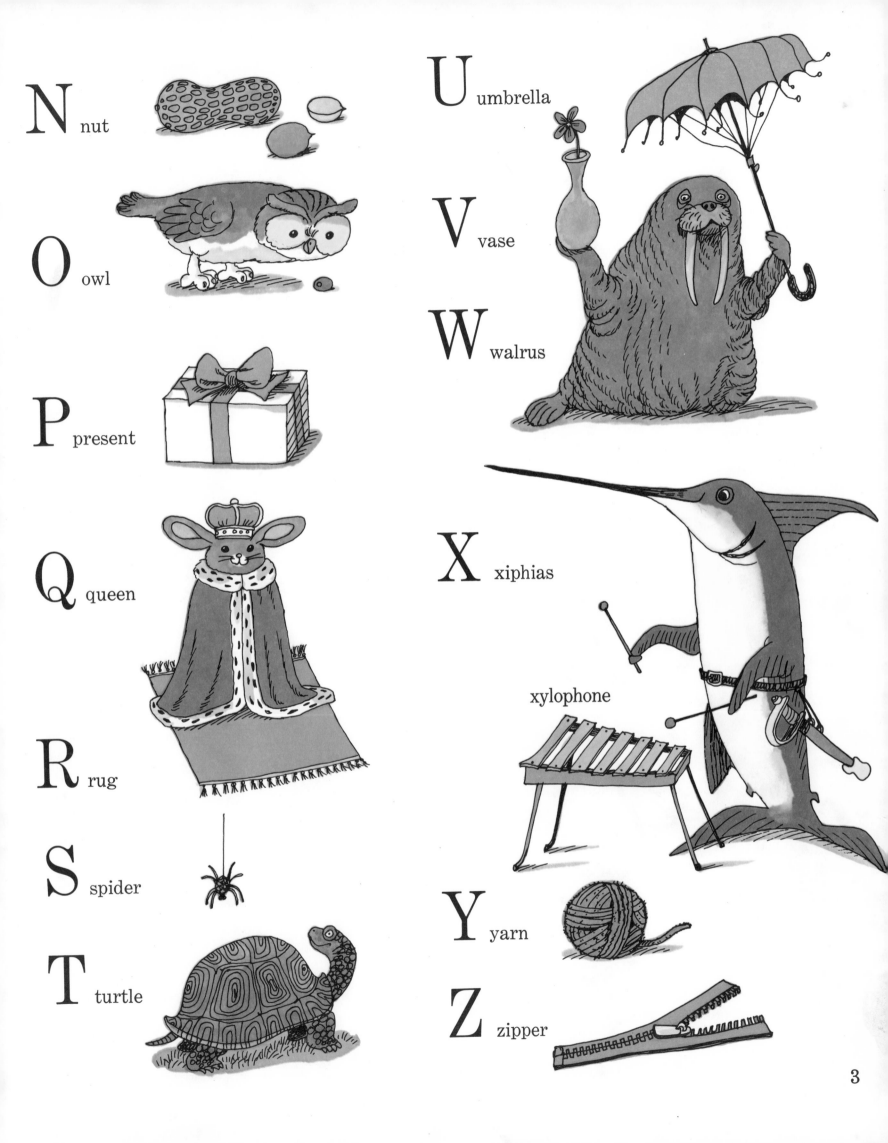

mosquito

moth

RICHARD SCARRY'S

BEST
WORD BOOK
EVER

mouse

moose

mushroom

moss

A Golden Book • New York
Western Publishing Company, Inc.
Racine, Wisconsin 53404

curtains

sun

window

THE NEW DAY

It is the morning of a new day.
The sun is shining.
Kenny Bear gets up out of bed.

washcloth

soap

towel

First he washes his
face and hands.

toothbrush

toothpaste

Then he brushes
his teeth.

mirror

comb

pajamas

He combs his hair.

shirt

pants

He dresses himself.

He makes his bed.

He goes to the kitchen
to eat his breakfast.

Kenny Bear sits in
his favorite chair.

He is very hungry.
This is what he eats—

cold fruit juice

warm cereal

with cream

pancakes

with butter and maple syrup

He doesn't eat
the toaster.

fried eggs

bacon

toast

muffins

honey

jam

hot cocoa

cool milk

and a waffle.

When he finishes eating breakfast he helps
wash and dry the dishes.

cup   saucer   plate   bowl   fork   knife   spoon   glass

jar   pitcher   frying pan   pot   pan   bottle   juice squeezer   glass

Now he is ready to play with his friends.   7

THE RABBIT FAMILY'S HOUSE

Father Rabbit, Mother Rabbit, and the
Rabbit children are getting ready for
the new day. Their friend Owl
is waiting for the children
to come outside.
Can you find him?

chimney

roof

mirror

lamp

bed

Big
Brother's
bedroom

cupboard

dining
room

kitchen

sink

Father

table

back door

stove

chair

fl

Mother

axe

woodpile

lawn

birdbath

WHOO

owl

smoke

antenna

light
switch

television set

record player

hassock

Mickey

bunk bed

bathroom

Molly

upstairs hall

bedroom

front door

living room

candle

outside
light

picture

telephone

fireplace

stairs

sofa or couch

front
hall

doormat

rug

window

stone walk

9

PAINTING AND DRAWING WITH COLORS

Painting and drawing are fun.
You can use bright colors.
You can paint with brushes
or even your fingers. You can
draw with crayons or pencils.
What do you like to draw?

paper

finger painting

make orange

make green

pencil

eraser

pencil drawing

make violet

make pink

make gray

make brown

water dish

watercolors

poster paint

LIBRARY WEEK

smock

paintbrushes

crayons

pastels

TOYS

Sometimes it is fun to play by yourself. Sometimes it is fun to play with your friends. What are your favorite toys? Do you like to play with blocks?

rocking horse

tricycle

electric trains

truck and loader

blocks

scooter

glider

robot

building set

croquet

AT THE PLAYGROUND

The children are all having fun doing different things. Which children are doing the things you like best?

seesaw

slide

leapfrog

somersault

hide-and-seek

ring-around-a-rosie

jump rope

ladder

rings

swing

sliding pole

top

roller skates

bubble blowing

kite

jungle gym

merry-go-round

tag

ring toss

hoop rolling

jacks

marbles

sandbox

kite string

bouncing ball

hopscotch

13

hammer

nail

TOOLS

Everyone is very busy
working with tools.
What tools do you have
in your house? What
would you like to build?

pushpin

axe

carpenter

board

sandpaper

ladder

saw

sawdust

hacksaw

log

drill

plane

vise

woodpecker

wood shavings

jigsaw

screwdriver

screws

pliers

file

14

bucksaw

trowel

bricklayer

hoe

brick wall

cement

brick

lumber

fence painter

paintbrush

ball of twine

sawhorse

barrel

paint

tack

tack hammer

hatchet

ruler

folding ruler

jackknife

toolbox

square

putty knife

shovel

bolt

nut

compass

dirt

wheelbarrow

pickaxe

monkey wrench

glue

15

silo

weather vane

scarecrow

crow

disc harrow

field

tractor

barn

hayloft

goat

tin can

milk can

stall

pail

farm truck

wagon

hen

rooster

baby chick

Kathy Bear is going
to feed the pig.

pigsty

corncrib

16

haystack

cow

apple tree

farmhouse

water pump

meadow

fence

sheep

horse

clothesline

apple

clothes basket

grass

THE BEARS' FARM

Kenny Bear is going to feed the chickens.

The Bears are working hard on their farm.
What are they all doing? What is the duck doing?
What is the scarecrow supposed to be doing?
He is not doing it, is he?

chicken coop

mailbox

well

duck pond

duck

ducklings

bee

pitchfork

beehive

17

weather instruments

blimp

microphone

control tower

AT THE AIRPORT

The air traffic controller is talking to the
pilot of the jet passenger plane. The controller
is giving the pilot take-off instructions.

baggage train

waiting
room

binoculars

tourist

camera

observation deck

jet plane

wind sock

runway

hangar

runway lights

light plane

propeller

mechanic

jet military plane

jet passenger plane

pilot

tail

cockpit

baggage handler

flight attendant

fuselage

wing

baggage
loader

jet engine

passenger-loading
stairs

hook

saw

ham

scales

wrapping paper

twine

meat cleaver

butcher

MEATS

pickl barr

bologna

frankfurters

hamburger

garbage pail

bacon

chop

fish

steak

a piglet who wants to work in the supermarket when she grows up

cart

sawdust

AT THE SUPERMARKET

The Pigs are buying groceries for their family.
What would you like to buy next time
you go to the market?
Would you like to buy
a pickle?

books

GOLDEN BOOKS

shopper

orange juice

raisins

customer

money

purse

eggs

milk

cashier

ice cream

butter

cash register

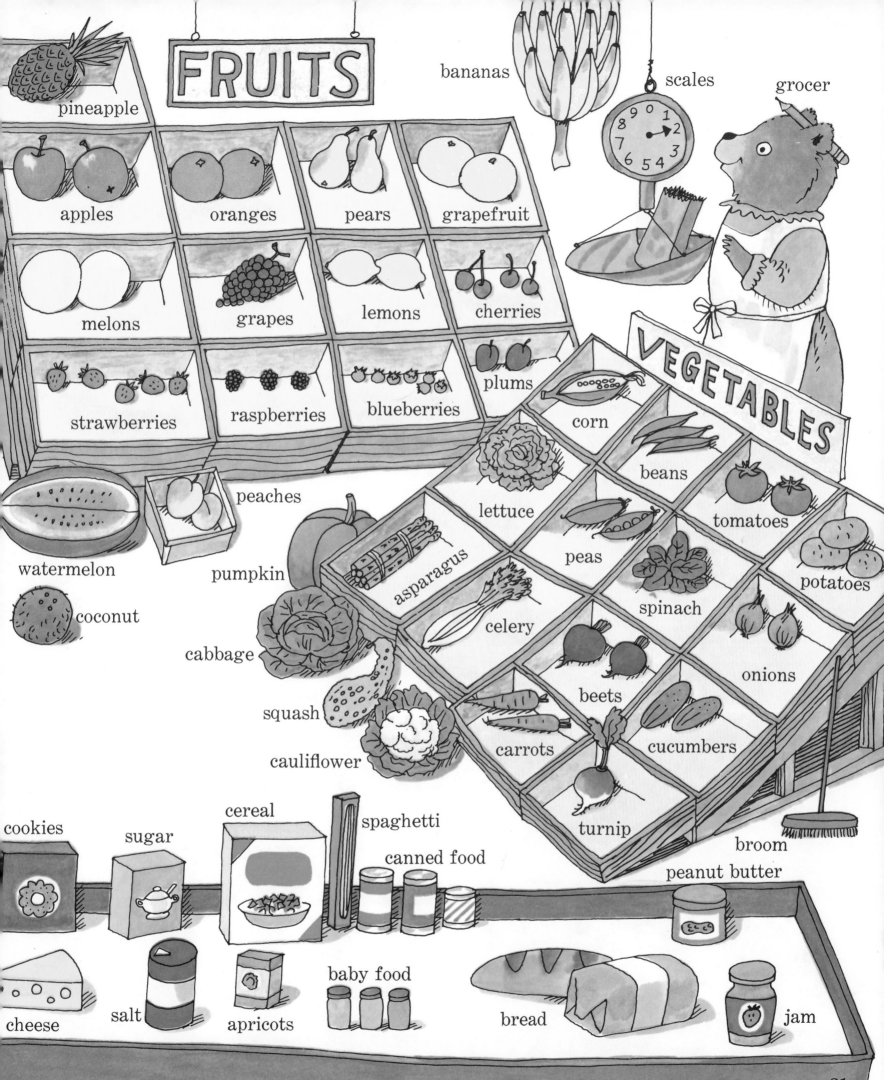

FRUITS

pineapple

apples

oranges

pears

grapefruit

melons

grapes

lemons

cherries

strawberries

raspberries

blueberries

plums

bananas

scales

grocer

peaches

watermelon

coconut

pumpkin

cabbage

squash

cauliflower

VEGETABLES

corn

lettuce

beans

peas

tomatoes

spinach

potatoes

celery

onions

beets

carrots

cucumbers

turnip

broom

cookies

sugar

cereal

spaghetti

canned food

peanut butter

cheese

salt

apricots

baby food

bread

jam

21

MEALTIME

The Pig Family is having a
special holiday meal. There
is so much good food to enjoy!
What do you see on the table
that you like to eat?

carving knife and fork

roast beef

meat platter

tablespoon

coffeepot

teapot

saltshaker

pepper shaker

fork

dinner plate

glass

cream pitcher

knife

cup

saucer

spoon

sugar bowl

napkin

turkey

cake

milk pitcher

green beans

gelatine

cranberry sauce

squash

baked potatoes

beets

onions

mashed potatoes

ice cream

peas

steak

butter

soup

pie

salad

rye bread

white bread

rolls

23

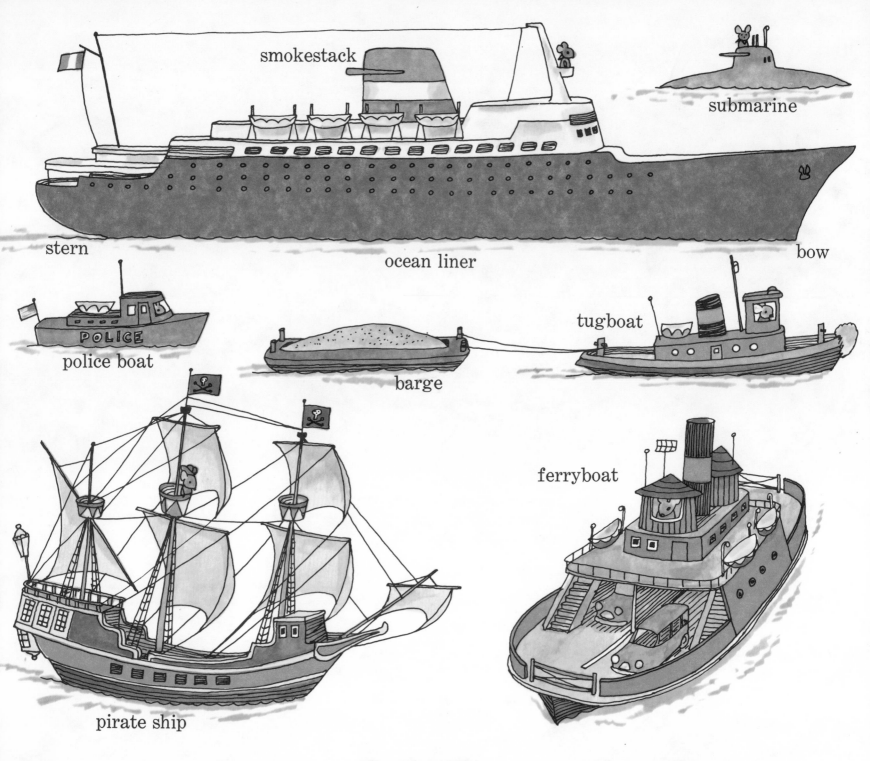

smokestack

submarine

stern

ocean liner

bow

police boat

barge

tugboat

pirate ship

ferryboat

BOATS AND SHIPS

One of the things in the water is not a boat, but it helps boats find the place they want to go. Do you know what it is?

motorboat

paddle

canoe

24

kayak

oar

rowboat

freighter

lightship

AMBROSE

coast guard ship

CG-7

oil tanker

fireboat

F.D.

fishing nets

fishing trawler

sport-fishing boat

speedboat

houseboat

raft

sailboat

THE WHITE SWAN

light buoy

2

25

KEEPING HEALTHY

Your doctors and your dentist are your good friends. They want you to stay healthy and strong. Will you give your doctors and dentist a big smile the next time you see them? How big a smile can you smile?

gauze bandage

adhesive tape

thermometer

stethoscope

cotton balls

tweezers

plastic bandage for small cuts and hurts

scissors

eye chart

flashlight

aspirin

pills

medicine

rubber hammer to make legs kick

tongue depressor for looking down throats

toothpaste

toothbrush

tooth

tooth with a cavity

dental tools

record chart to show where any cavities have been found

The X-ray machine can look inside your tooth to see if anything is wrong with it.

The doctor listens to your heart.

eye doctor

scales

hurt tail

The eye doctor tests your eyes.

doctor

patient

dental engine

dentist

rinse bowl

instrument table

water cup

dental unit

dentist's chair

dental hygienist

The dentist looks for cavities and the dental hygienist explains how to care for your teeth.

27

THE BEAR TWINS GET DRESSED

Kenny Bear awakens one cold, frosty morning.
He wants to dress very warmly before
going outside.

He yawns and gets up out of bed.
He takes off his pajamas, folds
them, and puts them in a dresser
drawer.

What should he wear today to keep warm?

 slippers

 pajama top

 pajama bottom

He puts on his

 T-shirt

 undershorts

 cap

 shirt

 pants

 overalls

 necktie

 sweater

 socks

 hat

 muffler

 sneakers

gloves

 jacket

 overcoat

 raincoat

and rainhat.

As Kenny is walking out of the front
door his father says, "Don't forget
to put your boots on!"

 boots

28

Kathy Bear stretches hard before she gets out of bed. She takes off her nightgown and hangs it on the hook in her closet.

What do you think Kathy should wear today to keep warm?

nightgown

She puts on her   underpants    undershirt    hair ribbon

 blouse    skirt   sweater   kneesocks   ear muffs   shoes

 snowsuit    and mittens.

She puts her change purse

 into her backpack.

As Kathy is walking out of the front door her mother says, "Don't forget to put your boots on!"

 Do you ever forget to put on your boots?

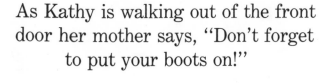

29

deer

lion

elephant

tiger

panda

monkeys

brown bear

gorilla

polar bear

30

buffalo

camel

zebra

zookeeper

giraffe

sea lion

leopard

The veterinarian makes sure all the animals are healthy.

zoo train

rhinoceros

AT THE ZOO

Mr. and Mrs. Mouse took
their children to the zoo.
How will those children
ever be able to get
all those balloons
into their house tonight?
Which is your favorite animal
at the zoo?

balloon seller

hippopotamus

BOOK PUBLISHER

COSTUMES

skyscraper

antenna

water tank

NEWSPAPER OFFICE

church

Dancing School

traffic light

Bookstore

apartment house

DRUGSTORE

telephone booth

mailbox

book reader

mail truck

letter car

street

IN THE CITY

Mouse has just bought a book at the bookstore.
She is going to buy a newspaper and then join
her rabbit friends at the sidewalk cafe and drink some
lemonade with them. Show with your finger the way
she will go. Remember to have her look both
ways before she crosses a street.

fire hydrant

32

hotel

street sign

park

park bench

statue

manhole

RESTAURANT

taxi

sidewalk cafe

barbershop

DANGER

one way

delivery cycle

traffic officer

police car

Mis

THEATER

CA

NOW PLAYING

BUS STOP

TAXI STAND

bus

SUBWAY

sidewalk

token seller

subway entrance

newspapers

subway station

newsstand

radio tower

ocean

island

A DRIVE
IN THE COUNTRY

There are many things to see when you take a drive
in the country. Can you see Harry and Sally,
the mountain climbers? Can you see what Harry
has dropped from his knapsack?

factory

lake

gas
station

tunnel

gas pump

tollbooth

turnpike or throughway
or superhighway

farm

bridge

mill

brook

stream

waterfall

34

picnic area

picnickers

lighthouse

fire lookout tower

beach

bay

crane

woods

seaport

drawbridge

hill

tug

mountain

village

windmill

river

pond

log cabin

mountain climbers

road

forest

cliff

knapsack

apple

35

HOLIDAYS

Holidays are happy times, aren't they?
Which holiday do you like best?
I bet you like them all.

On holidays we visit friends and relatives.
Sometimes we give or get presents.
What would you like to get for your birthday?

horn

New Year's Day

valentine

St. Valentine's Day

Easter

Easter egg

Easter bunny

Easter chick

balloons

rattle

cake

ice cream

Birthday

National Holiday

fireworks

flag

bugle

bass drum

fife

drum

uniform

ghost

Halloween

moon

skeleton

witch

black cat

witch's broom

pumpkin

Chanukah

trick-or-treat bag

angel

menorah

candle

Christmas

Christmas tree

wreath

holly

ornaments

tree lights

stockings

beard

fireplace

bag

Santa Claus

present

37

AT SCHOOL

School is fun. There are so many things we learn to do. Kathy Bear is learning how to find a lost mitten.

pencil

fountain pen

ball-point pen

paper

pencil sharpener

chalk

chalkboard eraser

notebook

eraser

straw

milk

ink

cookies

scissors

string

yarn

paper clip

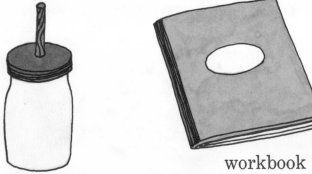

paste

workbook

storybook

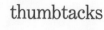

thumbtacks

modelling clay

lost-clothing drawer

flag

clock

bell

chalkboard

calendar

teacher

JANUARY

a b c

cat dog

map

map stand

inkwell

wastebasket

pupil

artist

desk

classroom

paper shapes

music teacher

refrigerator

kitchen cabinet

doorknob

can opener

soap

teapot

electrical outlet

counter

freezer

garbage pail

washing machine

dishwasher

Father Pig

laundry basket

eggbeater

eggshell

stool

Annie Pig

mixing bowl

batter
spoon

measuring cup

rolling pin

Susan
Pig

cookie cutter

dough

Peter
Pig

strainer

cake pan

funnel

cookie tray

spatula

ketchup
bottle

food grinder

flour bin
40

sugar bowl

mustard jar

closet

feather duster

broom

dustpan

mop

vacuum cleaner

egg timer

shelf

flyswatter

Mother Pig

hood

coffeepot

burner

teakettle

oven

stove

IN THE KITCHEN

iron

ironing board

All the Pigs like to work in the kitchen.
They are making good things to eat.
What is Father Pig making? What is
Mother Pig putting into the oven?

teaspoon

tablespoon

soup spoon

double boiler

blender

pestle   toaster

mortar

saucepan

corkscrew

ladle

colander

measuring spoons

matches

cutting board

electric mixer

potato masher

saltshaker

pepper grinder

cookbook

carving fork and knife

WHEN YOU GROW UP

What would you like to be when you are
bigger? Would you like to be a good
cook like your father? Would you like
to be a doctor or a nurse?

What would you like to be?

police officer

fire fighter

sailor

nurse

taxi driver

farmer

gardener

doctor   carpenter

musician

scientist

secretary

good cook

baker

dentist

42

singer

artist

pilot

fisherman

truck driver

teacher

garage mechanic

reporter

photographer

storekeeper

judge

librarian

dancer

daddy

mommy

THINGS WE DO

There are many things
that we can do. And there
are some things we cannot do.
What is one thing we can't do?
Look and see.

dig

blow

build

break

sleep

awaken

walk

run

stand

sit

read

watch

draw and write

44

pull

push

kick

talk

listen

shout

whisper

eat

laugh

smile

cry

jump over

crawl under

fall down

drink

we can't fly

peek

tip a hat

go up

go down

go in

come out

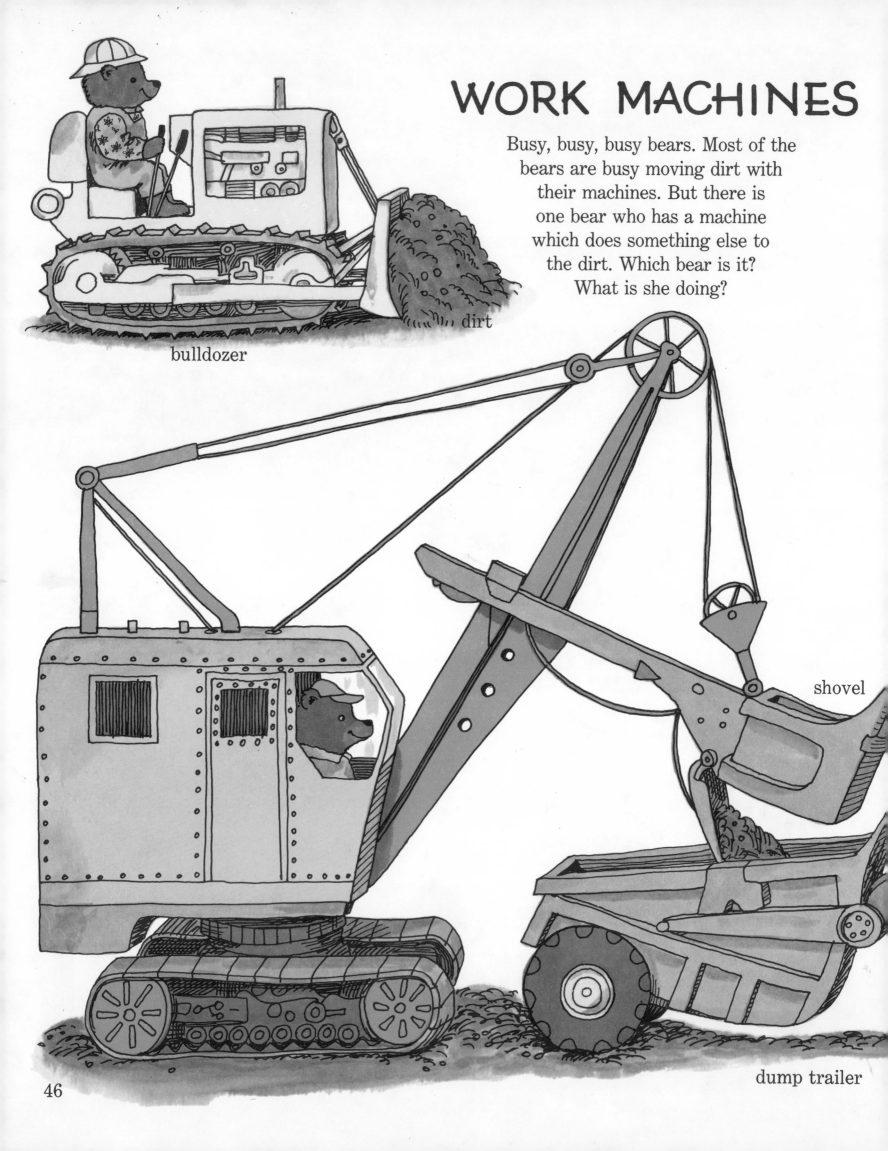

WORK MACHINES

Busy, busy, busy bears. Most of the bears are busy moving dirt with their machines. But there is one bear who has a machine which does something else to the dirt. Which bear is it? What is she doing?

dirt

bulldozer

shovel

dump trailer

tractor scraper

dump truck

tractor shovel

bucket loader

dirt

and tractor

roller

smooth dirt

rough dirt

47

automobile carrier

GASOLINE

gasoline truck

milk truck

broken-down car

tow truck

motorcycle

TAXI

TAXI

taxi

sports car

48

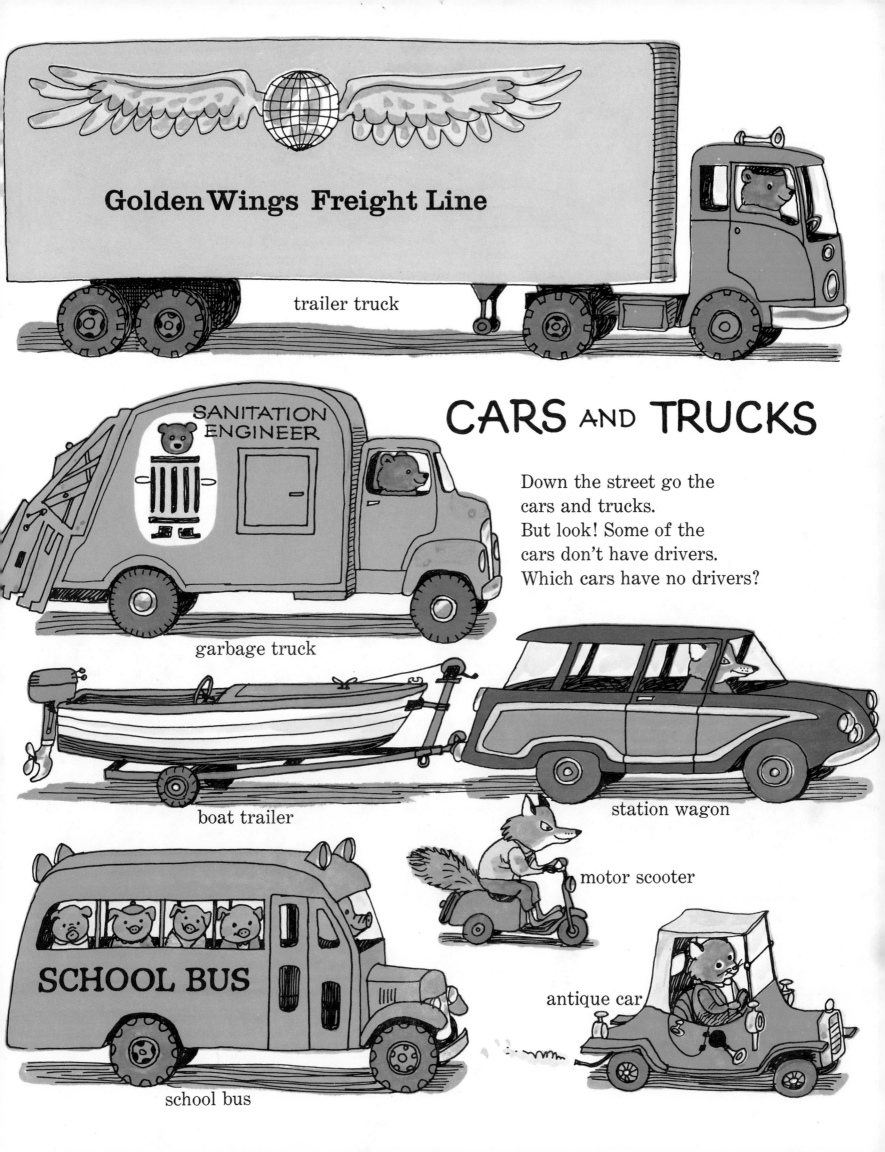

Golden Wings Freight Line

trailer truck

SANITATION ENGINEER

garbage truck

boat trailer

CARS AND TRUCKS

Down the street go the
cars and trucks.
But look! Some of the
cars don't have drivers.
Which cars have no drivers?

station wagon

motor scooter

antique car

SCHOOL BUS

school bus

round

square

triangle

diamond

star

crescent

heart

straight

curved

cone

SHAPES AND SIZES

big

fat

little

tiny

thin

tall

short

long

short

50

father

mother

THE BABY

The Cat family has a new baby kitten.
They don't know what to name it.
What would you like
to name the new baby?
Write the kitten's name here.

———— — — — — — — — — —

uncle

grandmother

bottle

baby

rattle

brother

aunt

sister

grandfather

diaper

playpen

cousin

high chair

crib

stroller

bassinet

play table

walker

baby carriage

51

AT THE CIRCUS

The band is playing and the animals are doing their acts. What do you like to watch best at the circus?

tent pole

balancing pole

tightrope performer

tightrope

band

bareback rider

bandstand

circus horse

rope ladder

performing elephant

sawdust

ring

ringmaster

trick dog

clown

pennant

circus tent

trapeze

trapeze artist

acrobat

safety net

ticket seller

hoop

lion

whip

cage

lion tamer

trained sea lion

popcorn seller

balloon seller

juggler

EDDIE

53

THE
FIRE FIGHTERS TO THE RESCUE

Will the brave fire fighters
put out the fire in time?
I think so, don't you?

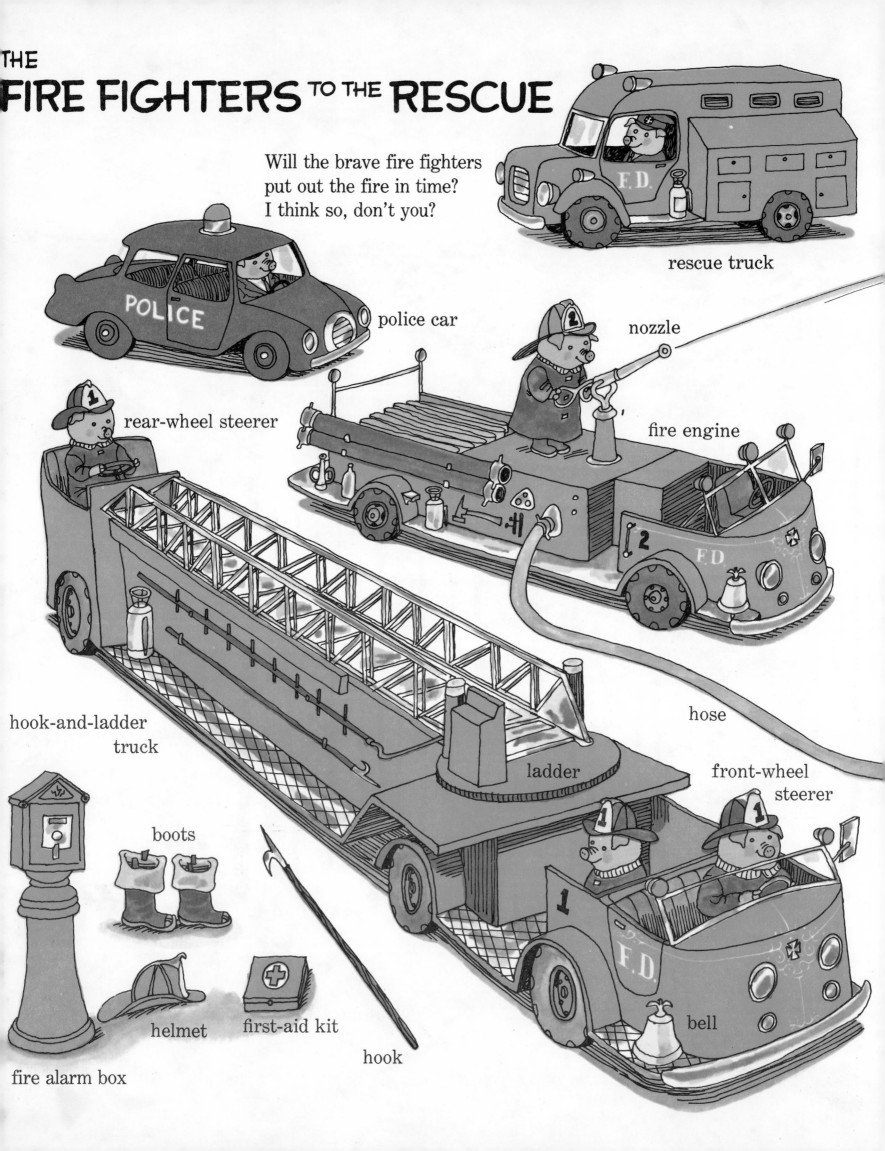

rescue truck

police car

rear-wheel steerer

nozzle

fire engine

hook-and-ladder
truck

ladder

hose

front-wheel
steerer

boots

helmet

first-aid kit

hook

bell

fire alarm box

ambulance

flames

water

smoke

fire chief

megaphone

cat in danger

fire chief's car

fire fighter

pumper

fire hydrant

ladder

fire fighters

rescue net

fire fighter

fire extinguisher

55

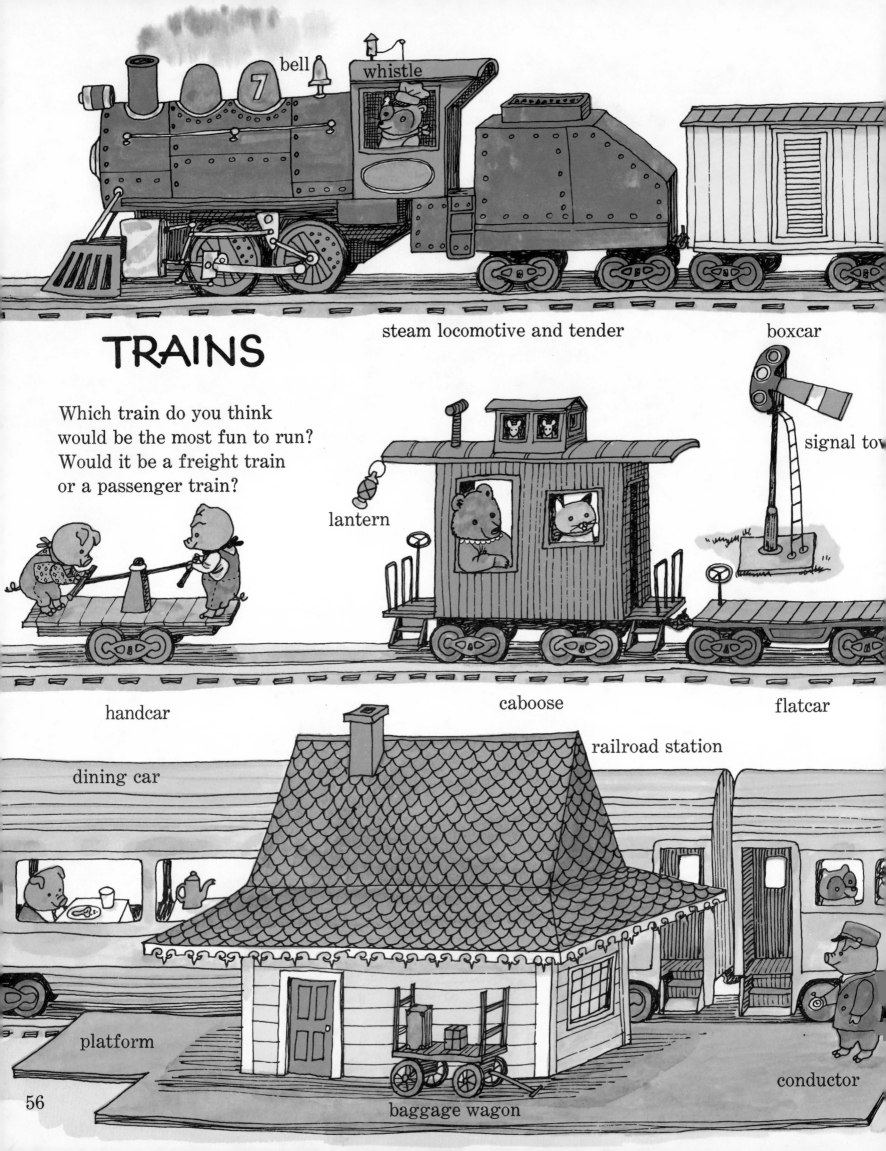

bell

whistle

TRAINS

steam locomotive and tender

boxcar

Which train do you think
would be the most fun to run?
Would it be a freight train
or a passenger train?

signal tow

lantern

handcar

caboose

flatcar

railroad station

dining car

platform

conductor

baggage wagon

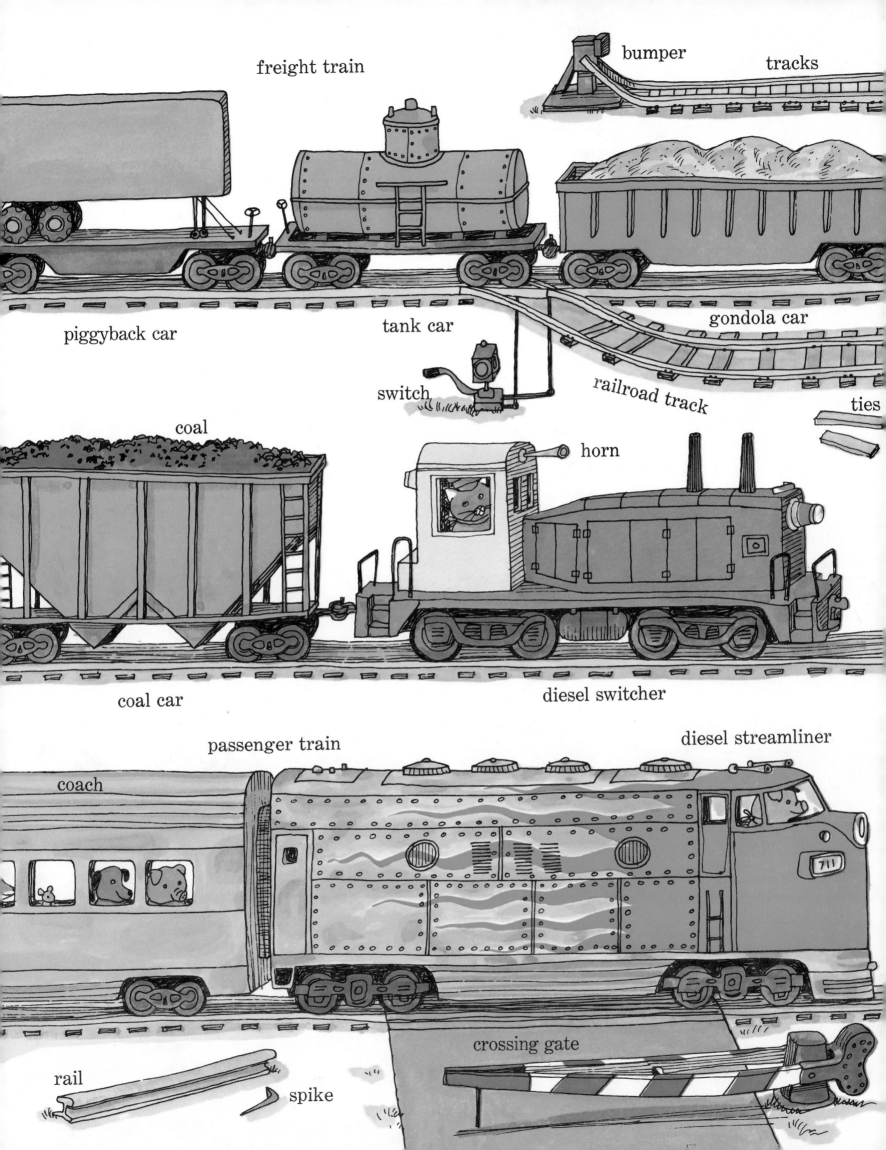

freight train

bumper

tracks

piggyback car

tank car

gondola car

switch

railroad track

ties

coal

horn

coal car

diesel switcher

passenger train

diesel streamliner

coach

711

crossing gate

rail

spike

AT THE BEACH

In the summertime it is fun
to go to the beach.
What do you think
Rabbit hears in the seashell?
Is it the sound of the waves?

telescope

lighthouse

summer cottage

oar

anchor

beach toy

shovel

rowboat

sandpiper

sand castle

waves

skate

bluefish

oyster

lobster

sea purse

scallop

hermit crab

clam

sea gull

umbrella

sun

pavilion

flagpole

sand dune

lifeguard

boardwalk

beach grass

stairs

bathhouse

beach chair

seashell

starfish

sand fort

waves

shrimp

minnow

horseshoe crab

crab

flounder

seaweed

mussel

59

MAKING THINGS GROW

Everyone is working in the garden.
Mr. Crow has a seed in his mouth.
Do you think he will plant it?
Or will he eat it?

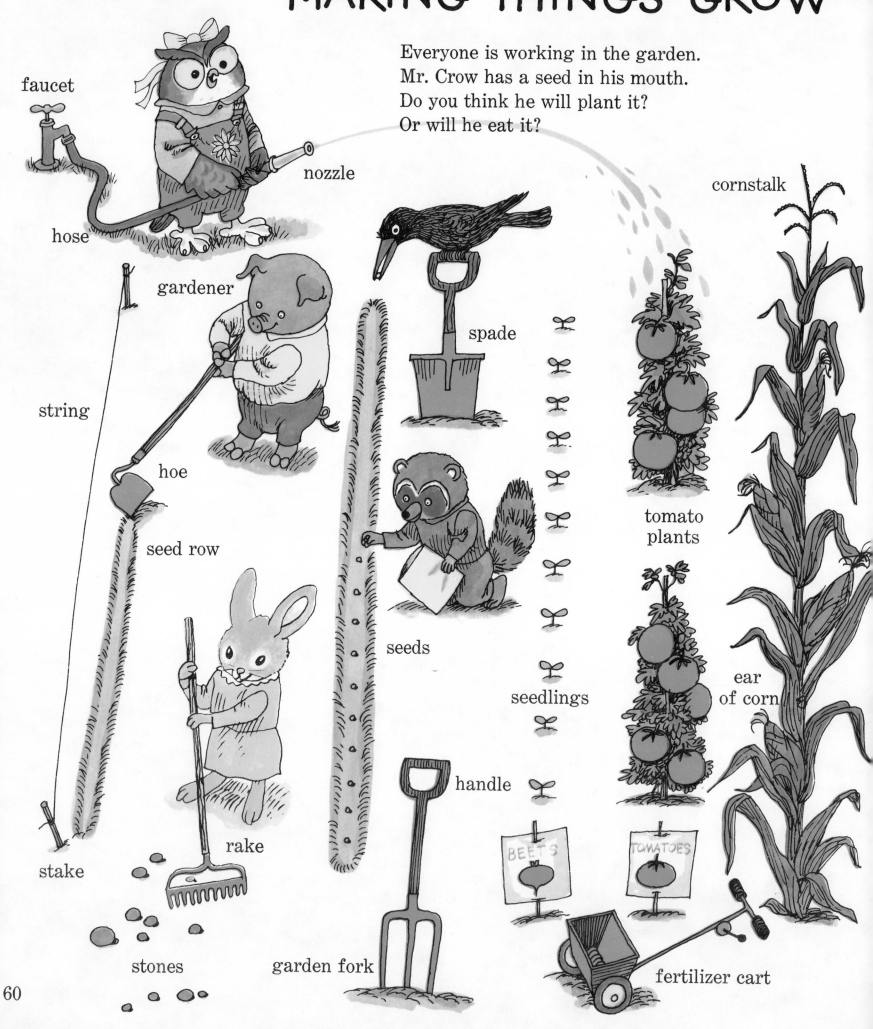

faucet

nozzle

hose

cornstalk

gardener

spade

string

hoe

seed row

seeds

tomato plants

stake

rake

stones

seedlings

handle

ear of corn

garden fork

BEETS

TOMATOES

fertilizer cart

60

THE WEATHER

sun

cloud

When we go outdoors we see what the weather is like. Sometimes it is sunny. Sometimes it is cloudy. It can be windy, or cold, or hot. It can be snowing or raining. What was the weather like outdoors today? What is your favorite kind of weather?

lightning

rain

hailstones

snowflakes

thermometer

rainbow

windmill

wind

hat

foxtail grass

raindrops

toad

a cat chasing a hat

toadstool

ladybug

puddle

mud

kite

rain shower

plow

robin

buds

nest

SPRING

Look at that baby lamb hop!
It is spring. She is happy.
Look at Mr. Bear coming out of
his cave! It is spring. He is happy.
Now he can use his new
lawn mower.

tree

lamb

bush

bridge

brook

fern

turtle

roots

cave

pussy willow

spring peeper

daffodil

lawn mower

crocus

violets

62

SUMMER

cow

meadow

calf

fence

cornfield

Do you like to go
on picnics in the summertime?
Ants just love to go to picnics.
Do you know why?

station wagon

tent

fly

screen

cooking grill

charcoal

picnic basket

cooler

hamburger

ketchup

charcoal bag

hotdog

pickle

mosquito

pole

paper cup

mustard

rock

ants

bobber

cattails

frog

dock

pond

water lily

dragonfly

pebbles

stones

63

sun

duck

falling leaves

gate

stone wall

corn shock

nuts

pumpkin

roadside stand

Indian corn

cider

jelly

squash

FALL

In the fall the air gets
colder. The green leaves turn to
bright colors. Then they fall to
the ground. Is that why we say
it is fall at this time of year?
Maybe it is.

smoke

basket of appl

flames

turkey

rake

bonfire

64

leaves

snowstorm

WINTER

There are many ways to have fun on the snow and ice. Maybe you would like to do all of them. Would you?

sleigh

icicle

fishing shack

skis

sled

toboggan

ice fishing

snow

ice-skating rink

ice skater

snowball

hockey stick

puck

ice skates

muffler

spare tire

jeep

snowplow

snowman

a pig all wrapped up

LITTLE THINGS

Here are many little things.
What little thing do you sometimes
put on your bedroom wall?

worm

dandelion seed

button

spool   thread

fly

ant   drop of water   ladybug   bead   snowflake   pin

fingerprint   petal   mosquito   butterfly   fishhook   crumb

bubble   peanut   tack   pen point   tea leaf   gumdrop   pea

caterpillar   jelly bean   firefly   ring   sand   blueberry

moth   rice   polliwog   keyhole   shell   marble   blade of grass

paper clip   cricket   raisin   beetle   raspberry   thimble   pincushion

hermit crab   pebble   sea horse   bee   mushroom   pearl   ink spot

confetti   feather   splinter   bean   safety pin   dot

baby mouse

66

PARTS OF THE BODY

Bears use their paws to pick things up.
What do you use?

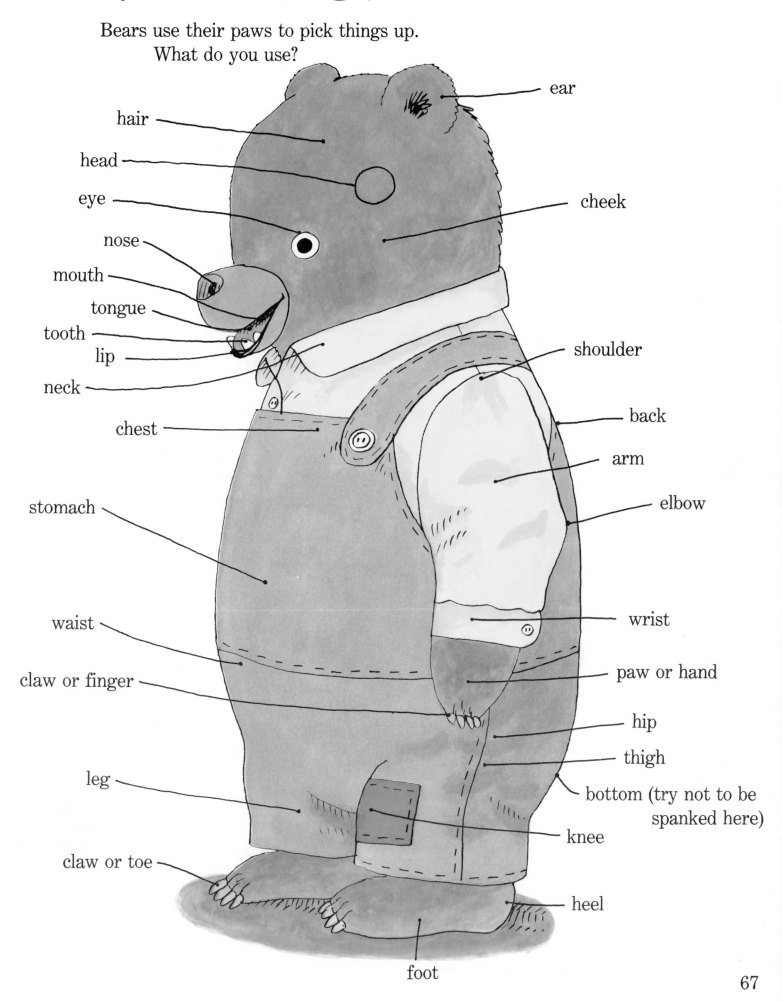

hair

head

eye

nose

mouth

tongue

tooth

lip

neck

chest

stomach

waist

claw or finger

leg

claw or toe

ear

cheek

shoulder

back

arm

elbow

wrist

paw or hand

hip

thigh

bottom (try not to be
spanked here)

knee

heel

foot

BEDTIME

Little Elephant is getting ready for bed.
But who is that hiding under the bed?
Find that rascal and tell her to brush her
teeth and get ready for bed, too.

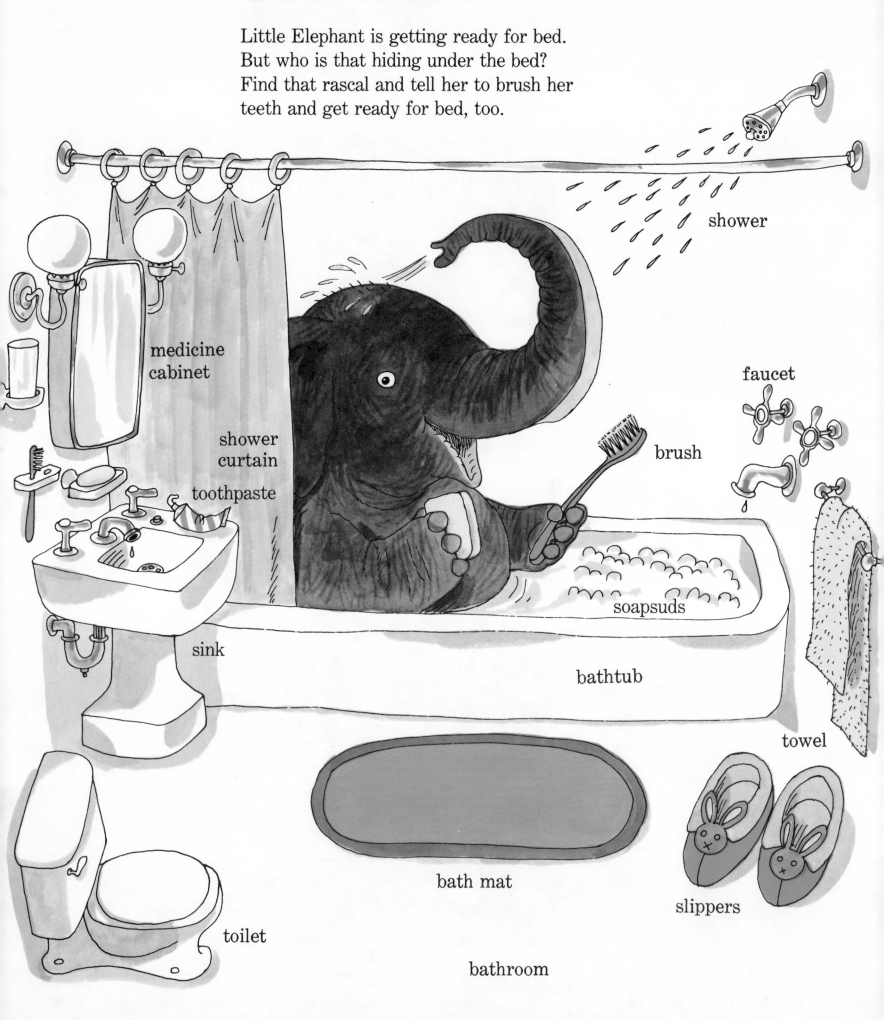

shower

medicine
cabinet

faucet

shower
curtain

brush

toothpaste

soapsuds

sink

bathtub

towel

toilet

bath mat

slippers

bathroom

NUMBERS

How high can you count?
Can you count up to
twenty ladybugs?
I'll bet you can.

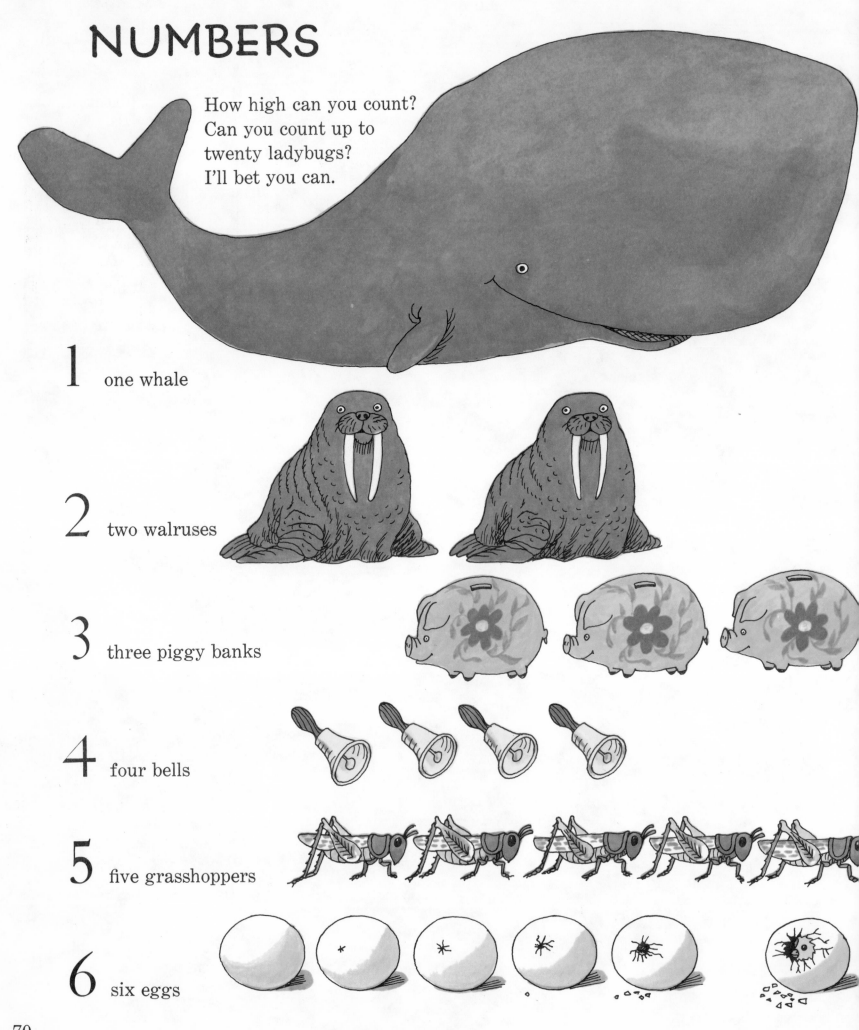

1 one whale

2 two walruses

3 three piggy banks

4 four bells

5 five grasshoppers

6 six eggs

7   seven caterpillars

8   eight spools

9   nine spiders

10   ten keys

11   eleven ants

12   twelve rings

13   thirteen gumdrops

14   fourteen leaves

15   fifteen snowflakes

16   sixteen acorns

17   seventeen pins

18   eighteen buttons

19   nineteen beads

20   twenty ladybugs